Thomas Bailey Aldrich

Mercedes

A drama in two acts

Thomas Bailey Aldrich

Mercedes
A drama in two acts

ISBN/EAN: 9783337343781

Printed in Europe, USA, Canada, Australia, Japan

Cover: Foto ©Andreas Hilbeck / pixelio.de

More available books at **www.hansebooks.com**

MERCEDES

A Drama in Two Acts

BY

THOMAS BAILEY ALDRICH

AS PERFORMED AT
PALMER'S THEATRE

BOSTON AND NEW YORK
HOUGHTON, MIFFLIN AND COMPANY
The Riverside Press, Cambridge
1894

CHARACTERS

ACHILLE LOUVOIS

LABOISSIÈRE

PADRE JOSÉF

MERCEDES

URSULA

SERGEANT & SOLDIERS

SCENE: SPAIN   PERIOD: 1810

CAST

CAPTAIN ACHILLE LOUVOIS }	*of* *the*	{ MR. E. J. HENLEY
LIEUTENANT LABOISSIÈRE }	*2d chasseurs*	{ MR. MAURICE BARRYMORE

PADRE JOSÉF . . . . . . MR. J. L. OTTOMEYER

MERCEDES . . . . MISS JULIA ARTHUR

OLD URSULA . . . MRS. D. P. BOWERS

Sergeants, Soldiers, etc.

MERCEDES

ACT I

A detachment of French troops bivouacked on the edge of the forest of Covelleda — A sentinel is seen on the cliffs overhanging the camp — The guard is relieved in dumb show as the dialogue progresses — Louvois and Laboissière, wrapped in greatcoats, are seated by a smouldering fire of brushwood in the foreground — Starlight.

Scene I

LOUVOIS, LABOISSIÈRE

LABOISSIÈRE

Louvois!

LOUVOIS, *starting from a reverie*

Eh? What is it? I must have slept.

Laboissière

With eyes staring at nothing, like an Egyptian idol! This is not amusing. You are as gloomy to-night as an undertaker out of employment.

Louvois

Say, rather, an executioner who loathes his trade. No, I was not asleep. I cannot sleep with this business on my conscience.

Laboissière

In affairs like this, conscience goes to the rear — with the sick and wounded.

Louvois

One may be forgiven, or can forgive himself, many a cruel thing done in the heat of battle;

but to steal upon a defenceless village, and in cold blood sabre old men, women, and children —that revolts me.

LABOISSIÈRE

What must be, must be.

LOUVOIS

Yes — the poor wretches.

LABOISSIÈRE

The orders are ——

LOUVOIS

Every soul !

LABOISSIÈRE

They have brought it upon themselves, if that comforts them. Every defile in these infernal mountains bristles with carabines ; every village gives shelter or warning to the guerrillas. The army is being decimated by assassination. It is the same ghastly story throughout Castile and Estremadura. After we have taken a town we lose more men than it cost us to storm it. I would rather look into the throat of a battery at forty paces than attempt to pass through certain streets in Madrid or Burgos after nightfall. You go in at one end, but, *diantre!* you don't come out at the other.

Louvois

What would you have? It is life or death with these people.

Laboissière

I would have them fight like Christians. Poisoning water-courses is not fighting, and assassination is not war. Some such blow as we are about to strike is the sort of rude surgery the case demands.

Louvois

Certainly the French army on the Peninsula is in a desperate strait. The men are worn out contending against shadows, and disheartened by victories that prove more disastrous than defeats in other lands.

Laboissière

It is the devil's own country. The very birds here have no song.[1] Even the cigars are damnable. Will you have one?

Louvois

Thanks, no.

[1] Except in a few provinces, singing-birds are rare in Spain, owing to the absence of woodland.

Laboissière, *after a pause*

This village of Arguano which we are to dis-
cipline, as the brave Junot would say, is it much
of a village?

Louvois

No; an insignificant hamlet — one wide *calle*
with a zigzag line of stucco houses on each side;
a *posada*, and a forlorn chapel standing like an
overgrown tombstone in the middle of the ceme-
tery. In the market-place, three withered olive
trees. On a hilltop overlooking all, a windmill
of the time of Don Quixote. In brief, the regu-
lation Spanish village.

Laboissière

You have been there, then? — with your three
withered olive trees!

Louvois, *slowly*

Yes, I have been there . . .

Laboissière, *aside*

He has that same odd look in his eyes which has puzzled me these two days. (*Aloud.*) If I have touched a wrong chord, pardon! You have unpleasant associations with the place.

Louvois

I? Oh no; on the contrary I have none but agreeable memories of Arguano. I was quartered there, or, rather, in the neighbourhood, for several weeks a year or two ago. I was recovering from a wound at the time, and the air of that valley did me better service than a platoon of surgeons. Then the villagers were simple, honest folk — for Spaniards. Indeed, they were kindly folk. I remember the old padre ; he was not half a bad fellow, though I have no love for the long-gowns. With his scant black soutane, and his thin white hair brushed behind his ears under a skull-cap, he somehow reminded me of my old mother in Languedoc, and we were good comrades. We used now and then to empty a bottle of Valdepeñas together in the shady posada garden. The native wine here, when you get it pure, is better than it promises.

Laboissière

Why, that was consorting with the enemy ! The Church is our deadliest foe now. Since the bull of Pius VII., excommunicating the Emperor, we all are heretical dogs in Spanish eyes. His

Holiness has made murder a short cut to heaven.[1] By poniarding or poisoning a Frenchman,
these fanatics fancy that they insure their infini-
tesimal souls.

LOUVOIS *rises*

Yes, they believe that; yet when all is said, I
have no great thirst for this poor padre's blood.
If the maréchal had only turned over to me some
other village! No — I do not mean what I say.
Since the work was to be done, it was better I

[1] In Andalusia, and in fact throughout Spain at that
period, the priests taught the children a catechism of
which this is a specimen: "How many Emperors of the
French are there?" "One actually, in three deceiving
persons."—"What are they called?" "Napoleon, Murat,
and Manuel Godoy, Prince of the Peace."—"Which is
the most wicked?" "They are all equally so." — "What
are the French?" "Apostate Christians turned heretics."
— "What punishment does a Spaniard deserve who fails
in his duty?" "The death and infamy of a traitor." —
"Is it a sin to kill a Frenchman?" "No, my father;
heaven is gained by killing one of these heretical dogs."

should do it. There's a fatality in sending me to Arguano. Remember that. From the moment the order came from headquarters I have had such a heaviness here. (*Pauses.*) Awhile ago, in a half doze, I dreamed of cutting down this harmless old priest who had come to me to beg mercy for the women and children. I cut him across the face, Laboissière! I saw him still smiling, with his lip slashed in two. The irony of it! When I think of that smile I am tempted to break my sword over my knee, and throw myself into the ravine yonder.

LABOISSIÈRE, *aside*

This is the man who got the cross for sabring three gunners in the trench at Saragossa! It is droll he should be so moved by the idea of killing a beggarly old Jesuit more or less. (*Aloud.*) Bah! it was only a dream, *voilà tout* — one of those villainous nightmares which run wild over these hills. I have been kicked by them myself many a time. What, the devil! dreams always go by contraries; in which case you will have the satisfaction of being knocked on the head by the venerable padre — and so quits. It may come to that. Who knows? We are surrounded by spies; I would wager a week's rations that Arguano is prepared for us.

Louvois

If I thought that! An assault with resistance would cover all. Yes, yes — the spies. They must be aware of our destination and purpose. A movement such as this could not have been made unobserved. (*Abruptly.*) Laboissière!

LABOISSIÈRE

Well?

LOUVOIS

There was a certain girl at Arguano, a niece
or god-daughter to the old padre — a brave girl.

LABOISSIÈRE

Ah — so? Come now, confess, my captain, it
was the *sobrina*, and not the old priest, you
struck down in your dream.

LOUVOIS

Yes, that *was* it. How did you know?

LABOISSIÈRE

By instinct and observation. There is always
a woman at the bottom of everything. You have
only to go deep enough.

LOUVOIS

This girl troubles me. I was ordered from Arguano without an instant's warning — at midnight — between two breaths, as it were. Then communication with the place was cut off. . . . I have never heard word of her since.

LABOISSIÈRE

So ? Did you love her ?

LOUVOIS

I have not said that.

LABOISSIÈRE

Speak your thought, and say it. I ever loved a love-story, when it ran as clear as a trout-brook and had the right heart-leaps in it. With this

wind sighing in the tree-tops, and these heavy
stars drooping over us, it is the very place and
hour for a bit of romance.　Come, now.

Louvois

It was all of a romance.

Laboissière

I knew it!　I will begin for you : You loved
her.

Louvois

Yes, I loved her.　It was the good God that
sent her to my bedside.　She nursed me day and
night.　She brought me back to life.... I know
not how it happened ; the events have no sequence
in my memory.　I had been wounded ; I dropped
from the saddle as we entered the village, and

was carried for dead into one of the huts. Then the fever took me. . . . Day after day I plunged from one black abyss into another, my wits quite gone. At odd intervals I was conscious of some one bending over me. Now it seemed to be a demon, and now a white-hooded sister of the Sacred Heart at Paris. Oftener it was that madonna above the altar in the old mosque at Cordova. Such strange fancies take men with gunshot wounds. One night I awoke in my senses, and there she sat, with her fathomless eyes fixed upon my face, like a statue of Pity. You know those narrow, melting eyes these women have, with a dash of Arab fire in them. . . .

LABOISSIÈRE

Know them? Sacrebleu!

Louvois

The first time I walked out, she led me by the hand, I was so very weak, like a little child learning to walk. It was spring, the skies were blue, the almonds were in blossom, the air was like wine. Great heaven! how beautiful and fresh the world was, as if God had just made it! From time to time I leaned upon her shoulder, not thinking of her.... Later I came to know her — a saint in disguise, a peasant-girl with the instincts of a duchess.

Laboissière

They are always like that, saints and duchesses — by brevet! I fell in with her own sister at Barcelona. Look you — braids of purple-black hair and the complexion of a

newly-minted napoleon.   I forget her name.
(*Knitting his brows.*)   Paquita . . . Mariquita?
It was something-quita, but no matter.

LOUVOIS

How it all comes back to me !   The wild foot-
paths in the haunted forest of Covelleda; the
broken Moorish water-tank, in the plaza, against
which we leaned to watch the gypsy dances; the
worn stone-step of the cottage, where we sat of
evenings with guitar and cigarette.   What simple
things make a man forget that his grave lies in
front of him!   (*Pauses.*)   There was a lover, a
contrabandista, or something — a fellow who
might have played the spadassin in one of Lope
de Vega's cloak-and-dagger comedies.   The
gloom of the lad, fingering his stiletto-hilt!

Presently she sent him to the right-about, him and his scowls—the poor devil.

LABOISSIÈRE

Oh, a very bad case!

LOUVOIS

I would not have any hurt befall that girl, Laboissiére!

LABOISSIÈRE

Surely.

LOUVOIS

And there's no human way to warn her of her danger!

LABOISSIÈRE

To warn her would be to warn the village — and defeat our end. However, no French messenger could reach the place alive.

Louvois

And no other is possible. Now you understand my misery. I am ready to go mad.

Laboissière

You take the thing too seriously. Nothing ever is so bad as it looks, except a Spanish *ragoût*. After all, it is not likely that a single soul is left in Arguano. The very leaves of this dismal forest are lips that whisper of our movements. The villagers have doubtless made off with that fine store of grain and aguardiente we so sorely stand in need of, and a score or two of the brigands are probably lying in wait for us in some narrow cañon.

Louvois

God will it so !

LABOISSIÈRE

Louvois, if the girl is at Arguano, not a hair of her head shall be harmed, though I am shot for it when we get back to Burgos!

LOUVOIS

You are a brave soul, Laboissière! Your words have lifted a weight from my bosom. Without your aid I should be powerless to save her.

LABOISSIÈRE

Are we not comrades, we who have fought side by side these six months, and lain together night after night with this blue arch for our tent-roof? Dismiss your anxiety. What is that Gascogne proverb? — "We suffer most from the ills that never happen." Let us get some rest; we have

had a rude day. . . . See, the stars have doubled
their pickets out there to the westward.

LOUVOIS

You are right ; we should sleep.   We march at
daybreak.   Good-night.

LABOISSIÈRE

Good-night, and *vive la France !*

LOUVOIS

Vive l'Empéreur !

LABOISSIÈRE *walks away humming*
" *Reposez-vous, bons chevaliers !* "

LOUVOIS, *looking after him*

There goes a light heart.   But mine . . . mine
is as heavy as lead.

SCENE II

LYRICAL INTERLUDE

Soldiers' Song

While this is being sung behind the scenes the guard is relieved on the cliffs. Louvois wraps his cloak around him and falls into a troubled sleep.

The camp is hushed; the fires burn low;

Like ghosts the sentries come and go:

Now seen, now lost, upon the height

A keen drawn sabre glimmers white.

Swiftly the midnight steals away —

Reposez-vous, bons chevaliers!

Perchance into your dream shall come

Visions of love or thoughts of home;

The furtive night wind, hurrying by,

Shall kiss away the half-breathed sigh,

And softly whispering, seem to say,

Reposez-vous, bons chevaliers!

Through star-lit dusk and shimmering dew

It is your lady comes to you!

Delphine, Lisette, Annette — who knows

By what sweet wayward name she goes?

Wrapped in white arms till break of day,

Reposez-vous, bons chevaliers!

In the course of the song the stage is gradually darkened and the scene changed.

ACT II

Morning — The interior of a stone hut in Arguano — Through the door opening upon the calle are seen piles of Indian corn, sheaves of wheat, and loaves of bread partly consumed — Empty wine-skins are scattered here and there among the cinders — In one corner of the chamber, which is low-studded but spacious, an old woman is sitting in an arm-chair and crooning to herself — At the left, a settle stands against the wall — In the centre of the room a child lies asleep in a cradle — Mercedes — Padre Joséf entering abruptly.

SCENE I

MERCEDES, *Padre* JOSÉF, *then* URSULA

Padre JOSÉF

Mercedes! daughter! are you mad to linger so?

MERCEDES

Nay, father, it is you who are mad to come back.

Padre JOSÉF

We were nearly a mile from the village when I missed you and the child. I had stopped at your cottage and found no one. I thought you were with those who had started at sunrise.

MERCEDES

Nay, I brought Chiquita here last night when I heard the French were coming.

Padre JOSÉF

Quick, Mercedes! there is not an instant to waste.

MERCEDES

Then hasten, Padre Joséf, while there is yet
time.   [*Pushes him towards the door.*

Padre JOSÉF

And you, child ?

MERCEDES

I shall stay.

Padre JOSÉF

Listen to her, Sainted Virgin ! she will stay,
and the French bloodhounds at our very heels !

MERCEDES, *glancing at Ursula*

Could I leave old Ursula, and she not able to
climb the mountain ?   Think you — my own
flesh and blood !

Padre JOSÉF

Ah, *cielo!* true. They have forgotten her, the cowards! and now it is too late. God willed it —*santificado sea tu nombre!* (*Hesitates.*) Mercedes, Ursula is old — very old ; the better part of her is already dead. See how she laughs and mumbles to herself, and knows naught of what is passing.

MERCEDES

The poor grandmother! she thinks it is a saint's day.   [*Seats herself on the settle.*

Padre JOSÉF

What is life or death to her whose soul is otherwhere? What is a second more or less to the leaf that clings to a shrunken bough? But you, Mercedes, the long summer smiles for such as you. Think of yourself, think of Chiquita. Come with me, child, come!

URSULA

Ay, ay, go with the good padre, dear. There is dancing on the plaza. The gitanos are there, mayhap. I hear the music. I had ever an ear for tambourines and castanets. When I was a slip of a girl, I used to foot it with the best in the cachuca and the bolera. I was a merry jade, Mercedes — a merry jade. Wear your broidered garters, dear.

MERCEDES

She hears music. (*Listens.*) No. Her mind wanders strangely to-day, now here, now there. The gray spirits are with her. (*To Ursula gently.*)

No, grandmother, I came to stay with you, I and Chiquita.   [*Crosses over to Ursula.*

Padre JOSÉF

You are mad, Mercedes.   They will murder you all.

MERCEDES

They will not have the heart to harm Chiquita, nor me, perchance, for her sake.

Padre JOSÉF

They have no hearts, these Frenchmen.   Ah, Mercedes, do you not know better than most that a Frenchmen has no heart?

[*Points to the cradle.*

MERCEDES, *hastily*

I know nothing.   I shall stay.   Is life so sweet to me?   Go, Padre Joséf.   What could save you if they found you here?   Not your priest's gown.

Padre JOSÉF

You will follow, my daughter?

MERCEDES

No.

Padre JOSÉF

I beseech you!

MERCEDES

No.

Padre JOSÉF

Then you are lost!

MERCEDES

Nay, padrino, God is everywhere. Have you not yourself said it? Lay your hands for a

moment on my head, as you used to do when
I was a little child, and go — go! [*Kneels.*

Padre JOSÉF

Thou wert ever a wilful girl, Mercedes.

MERCEDES

Oh, say not so; but quick — your blessing,
quick!

Padre JOSÉF

À Dios. . . .

He makes the sign of the cross on Mercedes' forehead,
and slowly turns away. Mercedes rises, follows him to
the door, and looks after him with tears in her eyes.
Then she returns to the middle of the room, and sits on
a low stool beside the cradle.

SCENE II

MERCEDES, URSULA

URSULA, *after a silence*

Has he gone, the good padre?

MERCEDES

Yes, dear soul.

URSULA, *reflectively*

He was your uncle once.

MERCEDES

Once? Yes, and always. How you speak!

URSULA

He is not gay any more, the good padre. He is getting old . . . getting old.

MERCEDES

To hear her! and she eighty years last San
Miguel's day!

URSULA

What day is it?

MERCEDES, *laying one finger on her lips*

Hist! Chiquita is waking.

URSULA, *querulously*

Hist? Nay, I will say my say in spite of all.
Hist? God save us! who taught thee to say hist
to thy elders? Ay, ay, who taught thee? . . .
What day is it?

MERCEDES, *aside*

How sharp she is awhiles! (*Aloud.*) Pardon,
pardon! Here is little Chiquita, with both eyes

wide open, to help me beg thy forgiveness. (*Bends over the cradle.*) See, she has a smile for grandmother. . . . Ah, no, little one, I have no milk for thee; the trouble has taken it all. Nay, cry not, dainty, or that will break my heart.

URSULA

Sing to her, *nieta*. What is it you sing that always hushes her? 'T is gone from me.

MERCEDES

I know not.

URSULA

Bethink thee.

MERCEDES

I cannot. Ah — the rhyme of The Three Little White Teeth?

> Ursula, *clapping her hands*

Ay, ay, that is it!

> Mercedes *rocks the child, and sings*

Who is it opens her blue bright eye,

Bright as the sea and blue as the sky ? —

> Chiquita !

Who has the smile that comes and goes

Like sunshine over her mouth's red rose ? —

> *Muchachita !*

What is the softest laughter heard,

Gurgle of brook or trill of bird,

> Chiquita ?

Nay, 't is thy laughter makes the rill

Hush its voice and the bird be still,

> *Muchachita !*

Ah, little flower-hand on my breast,

How it soothes me and gives me rest !

> Chiquita !

What is the sweetest sight I know ?

Three little white teeth in a row,

Three little white teeth in a row,

Muchachita !

As Mercedes finishes the song, a roll of drums is heard in the calle. At the first tap she starts and listens intently, then assumes a stolid air. The sound approaches the door and suddenly ceases.

SCENE III

LABOISSIÈRE, MERCEDES, *then* SOLDIERS

LABOISSIÈRE, *outside*

A sergeant and two men to follow me ! (*Mutters.*) Curse me if there is so much as a mouse left in the whole village. Not a drop of wine, and the bread burnt to a crisp — the *scélérats !* (*Appears at the threshold.*) Hulloa ! what is this ? An old woman and a young one

— an Andalusian by the arch of her instep and the length of her eyelashes ! (*In Spanish.*) Girl, what are you doing here?

MERCEDES, *in French*

Where should I be, monsieur?

LABOISSIÈRE

You speak French?

MERCEDES

Caramba ! since you speak Spanish.

LABOISSIÈRE

It was out of politeness. But talk your own jargon — it is a language that turns to honey on the tongue of a pretty woman. (*Aside.*) It was my luck to unearth the only woman in the place !

The captain's white blackbird has flown, bag and baggage, thank Heaven! Poor Louvois, what a grim face he made over the empty nest! (*Aloud.*) Your neighbors have gone. Why are you not with them?

MERCEDES, *pointing to Ursula*

It is my grandmother, señor; she is very old.

LABOISSIÈRE

So? You could not carry her off, and you remained?

MERCEDES

Precisely.

LABOISSIÈRE

That was like a brave girl. (*Touching his cap.*)

I salute valor whenever I meet it. Why have all the villagers fled?

MERCEDES

Did they wish to be massacred?

LABOISSIÈRE, *shrugging his shoulders*

And you?

MERCEDES

It would be too much glory for a hundred and eighty French soldiers to kill one poor peasant girl. And then to come so far!

LABOISSIÈRE, *aside*

She knows our very numbers, the fox! How she shows her teeth!

MERCEDES

Besides, señor, one can die but once.

LABOISSIÈRE

That is often enough. — Why did your people waste the bread and wine?

MERCEDES

That yours might neither eat the one nor drink the other. We do not store food for our enemies.

LABOISSIÈRE

They could not take away the provisions, so they destroyed them?

MERCEDES, *mockingly*

Nothing escapes you!

Laboissière

Is that your child?

Mercedes

Yes, the *hija* is mine.

Laboissière

Where is your husband — with the brigands yonder?

Mercedes

My husband?

Laboissière

Your lover, then.

Mercedes

I have no lover. My husband is dead.

LABOISSIÈRE

I think you are lying now. He's a guerrilla.

MERCEDES

If he were, I should not deny it. What Spanish woman would rest her cheek upon the bosom
that has not a carabine pressed against it this
day? It were better to be a soldier's widow
than a coward's wife.

LABOISSIÈRE, *aside*

The little demon ! But she is ravishing ! She
would have upset St. Anthony, this one — if he
had belonged to the Second Chasseurs ! What
is to be done ? Theoretically, I am to pass my
sword through her body; practically, I shall make
love to her in ten minutes more, though her

readiness to become a widow is not altogether pleasing. (*Aloud.*) Here, sergeant, go report this matter to the captain. He is in the posada at the farther end of the square.

Exit sergeant. Shouts of exultation and laughter are heard in the calle, and presently three or four soldiers enter, bearing several hams and a skin of wine.

1st Soldier

Voilà, lieutenant !

Laboissière

Where did you get that ?

2d Soldier

In a cellar hard by, hidden under some rushes.

3d Soldier

There are five more skins of wine like this

jolly fellow in his leather jacket. Pray order a division of the booty, my lieutenant, for we are as dry as herrings in a box.

LABOISSIÈRE

A moment, my braves. (*Looks at Mercedes significantly.*) Woman is that wine good?

MERCEDES

The vintage was poor this year, señor.

LABOISSIÈRE

I mean — is that wine good for a Frenchman to drink?

MERCEDES

Why not, señor?

LABOISSIÈRE, *sternly*

Yes or no?

MERCEDES

Yes.

LABOISSIÈRE

Why was it not served like the rest, then?

MERCEDES

They hid a few skins, thinking to come back for it when you were gone. An ill thing does not last forever.

LABOISSIÈRE

Open it, some one, and fetch me a glass. (*To Mercedes.*) You will drink this.

MERCEDES, *coldly*

When I am thirsty I drink.

LABOISSIÈRE

Pardieu! this time you shall drink because *I* am thirsty.

MERCEDES

As you will. (*Empties the glass.*) To the King.

LABOISSIÈRE

That was an impudent toast. I would have preferred the Emperor or even Godoy; but no matter — each after his kind. To whom will the small-bones drink?

MERCEDES

The child, señor?

LABOISSIÈRE

Yes, the child ; she is pale and sickly-looking ;
a draught will do her no harm.   All the same,
she will grow up and make some man wretched.

MERCEDES

But. señor ——

LABOISSIÈRE

Do you hear ?

MERCEDES

But Chiquita, señor — she is so little, only
thirteen months old, and the wine is strong !

LABOISSIÈRE

She shall drink.

MERCEDES

No, no !

LABOISSIÈRE

I have said it, sacré nom ——

MERCEDES

Give it me, then. (*Takes the glass and holds it to the child's lips.*)

LABOISSIÈRE *watching her closely*

Woman ! your hand trembles.

MERCEDES

Nay, it is Chiquita swallows so fast. See ! she has taken it all. Ah, señor, it is a sad thing to have no milk for the little one. Are you content ?

LABOISSIÈRE

Yes ; I now see that the men may quench their thirst without fear. One cannot be too cautious in this hospitable country ! Fall to, my children ; but first, a glass for your lieutenant.

[*Drinks.*

URSULA

Ay, ay, the young forget the old . . . forget the old.

LABOISSIÈRE, *laughing*

Why, the depraved old sorceress ! But she is right. She should have her share. *Place aux dames !* A cup, somebody, for Madame la Diablesse !

MERCEDES, *aside*

José-Maria!

One of the men carries wine to Ursula. Mercedes sits
on the stool beside the cradle, resting her forehead on
her palms. Laboissière stretches himself on the settle.
Several soldiers come in, and fill their canteens from
the wine-skin. They stand in groups, talking in under-
tones among themselves.

URSULA *rises from her chair*

The drink has warmed me to the heart, Mercedes! Said I not there was dancing on the
plaza? 'T is but a step from here. 'T would
do these old eyes good to look once more upon
the dancers. The music drags me yonder!
(*Wanderingly.*) Nay, take away your hands,
Mercedes — a plague upon ye!   [*Goes out.*

LABOISSIÈRE *suddenly starts to his feet and dashes his glass on the floor*

The child! look at the child! What is the

matter with it? It turns livid—it is dying! Comrades, we are poisoned!

MERCEDES *rises hastily and throws her mantilla over the cradle*

Yes, you are poisoned! *Al fuego — al fuego —todos al fuego!*[1] You to perdition, we to heaven!

[*The soldiers advance towards Mercedes.*

LABOISSIÈRE *interposing*

Leave her to me! Quick, some of you, go warn the others! (*Unsheathes his sword.*) I end where I ought to have begun.

MERCEDES *tearing aside her neckerchief*

Strike here, señor. . . .

[1] To the flames — to the flames — all of you to the flames!

Louvois *enters, and halts between the two with a dazed expression ; he glances from Laboissière to the woman, and catches his breath*

Mercedes !

Laboissière

Louvois, we are dead men ! Beware of her, she is a fiend ! Kill her without a word ! The drink already throttles me — I — I cannot breathe here.

[*Staggers out, followed wildly by the soldiers.*

Scene IV

LOUVOIS, MERCEDES

Louvois

What does he say ?

Mercedes

You heard him.

LOUVOIS

His words have no sense. (*Advancing towards her.*) Oh, why are you in this place, Mercedes?

MERCEDES, *recoiling*

I am here, señor ——

LOUVOIS

You call me señor — you shrink from me ——

MERCEDES

Because we Spaniards do not desert those who depend upon us.

LOUVOIS

Is that a reproach? Ah, cruel! Have you forgotten ——

MERCEDES

I have forgotten nothing. I have had cause

to remember all. I remember, among the rest, that a certain wounded French officer was cared for in this village as if he had been one of our own people — and now he returns to massacre us.

LOUVOIS

Mercedes !

MERCEDES

I remember the morning, nearly two years ago, when Padre Joséf brought me your letter. You had stolen away in the night — like a deserter ! Ah, that letter — how it pierced my heart, and yet bade me live ! Because it was full of those smooth oaths which woman love, I carried it in my bosom for a twelvemonth ; then for another twelvemonth I carried it because I hoped to give it back to you. (*Takes a paper from her bosom.*) See, señor, what slight things words are! (*Tears the paper into small pieces, which she scatters at his feet.*)

Louvois

Ah!

Mercedes

Sometimes it comforted me to think that you were dead. Señor, 't is better to be dead than false — and you were false!

Louvois

Not I, by all your saints and mine! It is you who have broken faith. I should be the last of men if I had deserted you. Why, even a dog has gratitude. How could I now look you in the face?

Mercedes

'T was an ill day you first did so!

LOUVOIS

Listen to me !

MERCEDES

Too many times I have listened.　Nay, speak
not ; I might believe you!

LOUVOIS

If I do not speak the truth, despise me ! Since
I left Arguano I have been at Lisbon, Irun,
Aranjuez, among the mountains — I know not
where ; but ever in some spot whence it was im-
possible to send you tidings.　A wall of fire and
steel shut me from you.　Thrice I have had
my letters brought back to me — with the
bearers' blood upon them ; thrice I have trusted
to messengers whose treachery I now discover.
For a chance bit of worthless gold they broke
the seals, and wrecked our lives !　Ah, Mercedes,

when my silence troubled you, why did you not read the old letter again! If the words you had of mine lost their value, it was because they were like those jewels in the padre's story, which changed their color when the wearer proved unfaithful.

MERCEDES

Aquilles!

LOUVOIS

Though I could not come to you nor send to you, I never dreamed I was forgotten. I used to say to myself: " A week, a month, a year —what does it matter? That brown girl is as true as steel!" I think I bore a charmed life in those days; I grew to believe that neither sword nor bullet could touch me until I held you in my arms again. (*The girl stands with her*

*hands crossed upon her bosom, and looks at him
with a growing light in her eyes.*)   It was the
day before yesterday that our brigade returned
to Burgos — at last! at last! O love, my eyes
were hungry for you! Then that dreadful order
came.   Arguano had been to me what Mecca
is to the Mohammedan — a shrine to be reached
through toil and thirst and death.   Oh, what a
grim freak it was of fate, that I should lead a
column against Arguano — my shrine, my Holy
Land !

Mercedes moves swiftly across the room, and kneeling
on the flag-stones near Louvois's feet begins to pick up
the fragments of the letter. He suddenly stoops and
takes her by the wrists.

Mercedes !

MERCEDES

Ah, but I was so unhappy ! Was I unhappy ?

I forget. (*Looks up in his face and laughs.*) It
is so very long ago! An instant of heaven would
make one forget a century of hell! When I hear
your voice, two years are as yesterday. It was
not I, but some poor girl I used to know who was
like to die for you. It was not I — I have never
been anything but happy. Nay, I needs must
weep a little for her, the days were so heavy to
that poor girl. And when you go away again, as
go you must——

LOUVOIS

I shall take you with me, Mercedes. Do you
understand? You are to go with me to Burgos.
(*Aside.*) What a blank look she wears! She
does not seem to understand.

MERCEDES, *abstractedly*

With you to Burgos? I was there once, in the

great cathedral, and saw the bishops in their golden robes, and all the jewelled windows ablaze in the sunset. But with you? Am I dreaming this? The very room has grown unfamiliar to me. The crucifix yonder, at which I have knelt a hundred times, was it always there? My head is full of unwonted visions. I think I hear music and the sounds of castanets, like poor old Ursula. Those cries in the calle — is it a merry-meeting? Ah! what a pain struck my heart then! O God! I had forgotten! (*Clutches his arm and pushes him from her.*) Have you drunk wine this day?

LOUVOIS

Why, Mercedes, how strange you are!

MERCEDES

No, no! have you drunk wine?

LOUVOIS

Well, yes, a cup without. What then? How white you are!

MERCEDES

Quick! let me look you in the face. I wish to tell you something. You loved me once ... it was in May ... your wound is quite well now? No, no, not that! All things slip from me. Chiquita — nay, hold me closer, I do not see you. Into the sunlight — into the sunlight !

LOUVOIS

She is fainting!

MERCEDES

I am dying — I am poisoned. The wine was drugged for the French. I was desperate. Chiquita — there in the cradle — she is dead — and I ——   *[Sinks down at his feet.*

Louvois, *stooping over her*

Mercedes! Mercedes!

After an interval a measured tramp is heard outside. A sergeant with a file of soldiers in disorder enters the hut.

SCENE V

SERGEANT *and* SOLDIERS

1ST SOLDIER

Behold! he has killed the murderess.

2D SOLDIER

If she had but twenty lives now!

3D SOLDIER

That would not bring back the brave Laboissière and the rest.

2D SOLDIER

Sapristi, no! but it would give us life for life.

4TH SOLDIER

Miséricorde! are twenty ——

SERGEANT

Hold your peace, all of you! (*Advances and salutes Louvois, who is half kneeling beside the body of the woman.*) My captain! (*Aside.*) He does not answer me. (*Lays his hand hurriedly on Louvois's shoulder, and starts.*) Silence, there! and stand uncovered. He is dead!

CURTAIN.